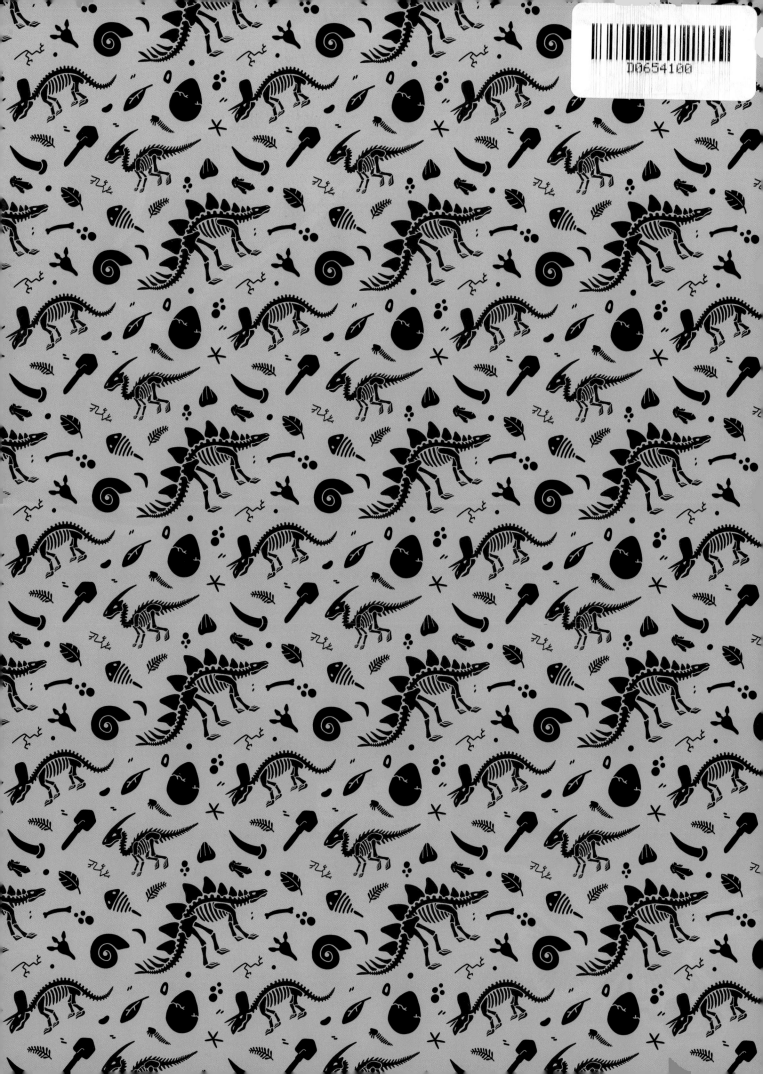

Farshore

First published in Great Britain 2021 by Farshore
An imprint of HarperCollins*Publishers*
1 London Bridge Street, London SE1 9GF
www.farshore.co.uk

HarperCollins*Publishers*
1st Floor, Watermarque Building, Ringsend Road
Dublin 4, Ireland

Written by Claire Philip
Edited by Thomas McBrien
Designed by Martin Aggett & Jessica Coomber
Images used under license from Shutterstock.com

© The Trustees of the Natural History Museum, London

ISBN 978 0 4555 0352 0
Printed in Romania

002

Parental guidance is advised for all craft and colouring activities.
Always ask an adult to help when using glue, paint and scissors.
Wear protective clothing and cover surfaces to avoid staining.

A CIP catalogue record for this title is available from the British Library.

Farshore takes its responsibility to the planet and its inhabitants very seriously. We aim to use papers from
well-managed forests run by responsible suppliers.

MIX
Paper from
responsible sources
FSC® C007454

FSC ™ is a non-profit international organisation established to promote
the responsible management of the world's forests. Products carrying the
FSC label are independently certified to assure consumers that they come
from forests that are managed to meet the social, economic and
ecological needs of present and future generations,
and other controlled sources.

Find out more about HarperCollins and the environment at
www.harpercollins.co.uk/green

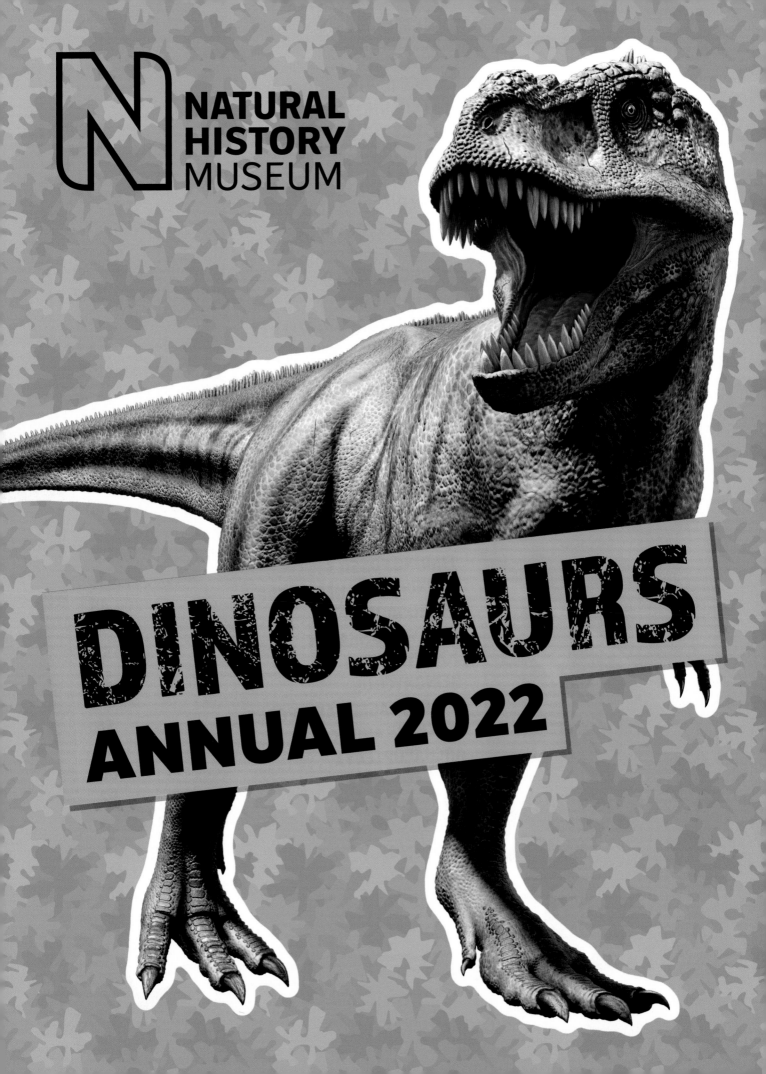

NATURAL HISTORY MUSEUM

DINOSAURS
ANNUAL 2022

CONTENTS

Packed full of fun facts and awesome activities!

NATURAL HISTORY MUSEUM

DINOSAURS
ANNUAL 2022

This book belongs to

....

....

Write your name here

Turn the page to turn back time.
Get ready to meet the dinosaurs!

AGE OF THE DINOSAURS

Magnificent creatures called dinosaurs once ruled the planet!

Reptile Relatives

Dinosaurs are an incredible group of reptiles that first lived on Earth around 245 million years ago. They lived for 170–180 million years through time periods called the Triassic, the Jurassic and the Cretaceous.

HOW DO WE KNOW?

As there are no dinosaurs alive today, scientists have to study their bones, eggs, nests, footprints — even their poo! — to learn about them. When a new discovery is made, experts look for evidence to prove, or disprove, ideas about how they lived and behaved.

ALL SHAPES AND SIZES

There were many kinds of dinosaur, both big and small. They could survive in lots of different habitats, from wide open plains to dense forests. Just like animals today, they were perfectly suited for their environments.

Coelophysis

Triassic Period

252–201 Million Years Ago
Dinosaurs first walked Earth

DID YOU KNOW?

Humans have only lived on Earth for a few hundred thousand years — that's much less than the dinosaurs!

CONTINENTAL DRIFT

Fossils from the same kinds of dinosaur have been discovered on different continents. This could be proof that Earth's continents were once joined up as one supercontinent.

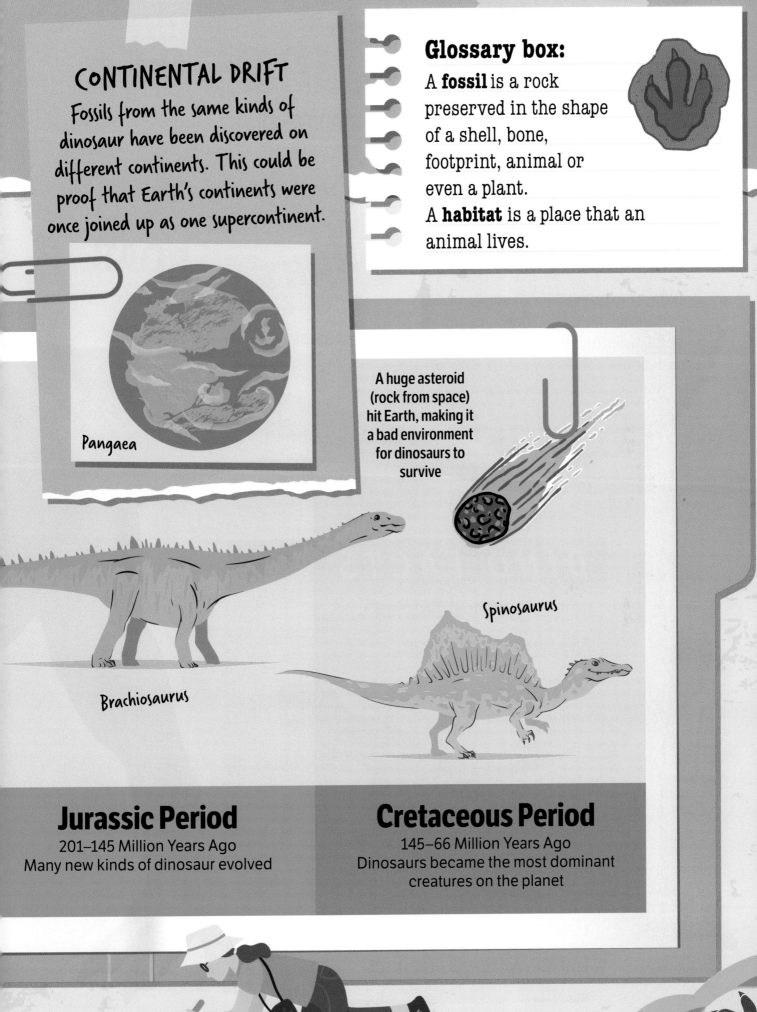

Pangaea

A huge asteroid (rock from space) hit Earth, making it a bad environment for dinosaurs to survive

Spinosaurus

Brachiosaurus

Jurassic Period
201–145 Million Years Ago
Many new kinds of dinosaur evolved

Cretaceous Period
145–66 Million Years Ago
Dinosaurs became the most dominant creatures on the planet

TYRANNOSAURUS REX

The most famous dino of all.

Expert hunter

Racing across the land on two strong legs, T-rex was an expert hunter. It had an excellent sense of smell, which helped it track down smaller dinosaurs to eat. This carnivore probably feasted on animals that had already died too.

SNORT

ROAR

DINO FACTS

Name: *Tyrannosaurus rex*

Meaning: *"Tyrant lizard"*

Size comparison:

Food: *Meat*

Danger rating: *10/10*

Habitat: *Swamps and forests*

Glossary box:
A **carnivore** eats other animals, while a **herbivore** eats plants.

Deadly bite

T-rex's mouth was full of razor-sharp teeth, so it could easily slice through bone. Its longest tooth was around 30cm (12in) long and shaped like a banana.

Powerful jaws that could open wide to swallow prey

Short but strong arms

Tiny arms

Even though T-rex had short forearms compared to its body size, its grip would have been almost impossible to escape!

Walked upright on two legs

Dino Close-Ups

Which of these close-ups doesn't belong to a T-rex?

1   **2**   **3**

Answers on page 69.

SPOT THE DIFFERENCE!

How quickly can you spot the ten differences between the pictures?

A

Set a timer and see how long it takes you to spot the differences!

It took me [ ] minutes and [ ] seconds to find all the differences.

12

B

Answers on page 69.

Circle each difference you find. Colour in the eggs as you go.

DIPLODOCUS

One of the longest dinos ever discovered.

Did You Know?

Diplodocus was around 26m (85ft) long – that's a little longer than the height of the Statue of Liberty! Its tail made up an amazing 6m (20ft) of its length and was used like a whip to knock away predators.

Long neck

Front legs shorter than back legs

Tiny head

Safety First

This dino may have laid its eggs on the ground, buried under leaf litter. When the eggs hatched, the dead plants would have protected the babies from predators.

DINO FACTS

Name: *Diplodocus*

Meaning: *"Double beam"*

Size comparison:

Food: *Plants*

Danger rating: *3/10*

Habitat: *Sparse woodland and plains*

CHOMP

Glossary box:
Predators are animals that hunt other animals (their **prey**).

Whip-like tail

Dinner time!

Diplodocus used its super long neck to reach leaves from the tops of trees. It may have even reared up on its back legs to gain extra height. Diplodocus had to eat tonnes of plant-matter every day to stop it from going hungry.

True or False?

Diplodocus hunted other smaller dinosaurs to eat.

true ◯   false ◯

Answers on page 69.

DINOSAUR DOODLES!

It's time to draw! Follow the instructions to finish this dinosaur scene.

Instructions

- Draw more fern leaves.
- Add extra flying reptiles.
- Draw clouds in the sky.
- Add some dinosaur eggs to the plants.

COLOUR BY NUMBER

This T-rex needs colouring in!
Use the colour key to complete this dinosaur picture.

WHAT'S YOUR NAME?

How do scientists name dinosaurs?

BODY PARTS

Dinosaurs are often named after their most noticeable body feature. For example, the name Deinonychus means "terrible claw" and it's easy to see why! These lightweight predators are thought to have hunted their prey in packs, using their sharp claws to attack.

FOSSIL HUNTER

Some dinos have been named after people. Lambeosaurus was named after the famous fossil expert who gave Stegosaurus, Chasmosaurus and Edmontosaurus their names.

Long tail

Lawrence Lambe

WORLD TRAVELLERS

Dinosaurs are also named after where they were discovered. Utahraptor is named after the place in which it was found — Utah, USA. Can you guess where Denversaurus was found?

GUESS THE NAME!

In 2019, the fossil remains of a previously unknown dinosaur were discovered in the UK. Scientists discovered large air-filled spaces in the fossilised bone.

Can you guess what they named the dino?

A. Dainty biter

B. Light-footed prancer

C. Tip-toed walker

D. Air-filled hunter

Air-filled lungs

Short arms

Answers on page 69.

19

VELOCIRAPTOR

This infamous hunter is known for its speed.

DINO FACTS

Name: *Velociraptor*

Meaning: *"Quick plunderer"*

Size comparison:

Food: *Meat*

Danger rating: *8/10*

Habitat: *Deserts and scrublands*

Hawk-eyed Hunter

These intelligent dinosaurs had excellent eyesight, which they used to spot prey such as small mammals and even other dinosaurs.

Did You Know

Velociraptors were extremely agile, reaching possible speeds of up to 40mph (60km/h). Once they caught up with their prey, they used their sharp claws to bring it to the ground. They may have hunted in groups to prey on larger animals.

Warm Feathers

Experts believe that Velociraptors were covered in feathers, though unlike most birds, they could not fly. Their feathers may have helped them keep a steady body temperature.

Large eyes

Small body

Feathered arms and tail

Large claw on second toe

Track the Trail

Track the correct trail left behind by this super-fast Velociraptor.

A
B
C
D

Answers on page 69.

WINGS VS TAILS

Who can reach the finish line first?
Roll your dice to find out!

RULES

1. Roll the dice to move your counter across the board.

2. If you land on a feather, skip forwards 2 squares.

3. If you land on a reptile, skip backwards 3 squares.

4. The winner is the first person to reach the final square!

YOU WILL NEED

- 2-4 players
- One dice
- 1 counter per player

FINISH

48

47

46 go back 3

33

34

35

32

31 go back 3

30

17 go forward 2

18

19

16

15

14 go forward 2

START

1

2

3

45

44

43

42 go forward 2

41

36

37 go back 3

38

39

40

29

28

27

26

25 go forward 2

20

21

22 go back 3

23

24

13

12

11

10

9

4 go back 3

5

6

7 go forward 2

8

23

ALLOSAURUS

This dino was a powerful, meat-eating predator.

Did You Know

This large, deadly dinosaur grew up to 10.5m (35ft) long. Fossil remains suggest that it hunted dinosaurs as large as Diplodocus, which grew to 26m (85ft)!

Mini T-rex:

Although it looked similar to a T-rex, Allosaurus had a much lighter build – and longer arms! It lived in the Late Jurassic Period, almost 90 million years before T-rex, which lived in the Late Cretaceous Period.

DINO FACTS

Name: *Allosaurus*

Meaning: *"Other lizard"*

Size comparison:

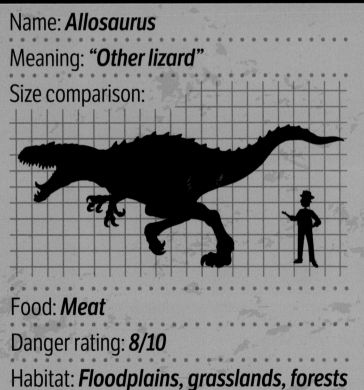

Food: *Meat*

Danger rating: *8/10*

Habitat: *Floodplains, grasslands, forests*

Sharp teeth

Gripping claws

Jaw-some!

Experts believe it slashed its prey with its saw-like teeth rather than chomping down hard, like other dinos. Allosaurus would open its mouth extremely wide, then attack.

A jaw that could open extremely wide

Other Lizard

Allosaurus was given its name ("other lizard") simply because it was different to any other dinosaur that had been discovered so far!

WHOOSH

Long Tail

Dino Dot-to-Dot

Join the dots to finish this dinosaur picture, then colour it in!

PREHISTORIC PUZZLERS

Very punny! Can you work out the answers to these dino jokes?

Answers on page 69.

1 What do you call a dinosaur with an amazing vocabulary?

2 What is the scariest kind of dinosaur?

It's all pun and games!

3 How does Triceratops sit?

26

4 What do dinosaurs say when they fall in love?

Ha! Ha!

5 What do you call a dinosaur that always makes jokes?

6 What do you call an anxious dinosaur?

PALAEONTOLOGISTS

Palaeontologists are scientists that study ancient life, including dinosaurs.

FINDING CLUES

Palaeontologists look for and study fossils to find out how different lifeforms have changed over time. Their discoveries give us clues about what our planet was like long ago.

KEEP NOTE

Record-keeping is an important part of a palaeontologist's job. They spend lots of time writing detailed descriptions of their fossil finds, comparing them to other fossils and even drawing pictures of them.

SPECIAL TRIPS

Palaeontologists go on expeditions to sites all around the world to search for fossils. Using their tools, they carefully take the fossils from the ground, then bring them back to the lab to study for clues.

Could you be a palaeontologist?

It takes a special kind of person to become
a palaeontologist. Do you have what it takes?
Circle your answers to find out!

Are you adventurous?	YES / NO
Do you love history?	YES / NO
Do you like going on expeditions?	YES / NO
Do you love dinosaurs and prehistoric creatures?	YES / NO
Do you want to be a scientist?	YES / NO

If you answered YES
to the questions above,
you could be a good fit
for the job!

29

SARCOSUCHUS

This prehistoric creature ambushed its prey.

River monster:

Sarchosuchus is one of the largest crocodile-like creatures that ever lived. This giant swam and hunted in the rivers of North Africa more than 100 million years ago.

Super-Croc:

It is thought that Sarcosuchus could grow to an almighty 12m (40ft) in length – that's as long as a bus! Modern saltwater crocodiles only reach half that length, topping out at 6m (20ft) long.

Hidden in the depths:

Sarchosuchus's eyes moved up and down rather than from left to right. This indicates that it swam just below the water's surface, hiding from its prey until the very last moment!

DINO FACTS

Name: *Sarcosuchus*

Meaning: *"Flesh crocodile"*

Size comparison:

Food: *Meat*

Danger rating: *7/10*

Habitat: *Rivers and riverbanks*

All Mixed Up

A

B

C

Can you find the missing jigsaw piece to complete the Sarcosuchus?

Answers on page 69.

Bowl-like end to snout

Powerful body

Upward-facing eyes

Mouthful of sharp teeth

SNAP

A-MAZE-ING DISCOVERY!

Help the palaeontologist reach the excavation site by solving the maze.
Can you collect all the fossils on your way?

FINISH

MAIASAURA

MUNCH!

Unlike many dinos, Maiasaura cared for its young.

Small head crest

Beaky Biter:

Maiasaura was a plant-eating duck-billed dinosaur. It had a bill that it used to snip plants, and lots of teeth to chew and grind the leaves.

Wide bill

DINO FACTS

Name: *Maiasaura*

Meaning: *"Good mother lizard"*

Size comparison:

Food: *Plants*

Danger rating: *3/10*

Habitat: *Grassland and wooded areas*

Dino Mother:

Maiasaura was given a name that means "good mother lizard" because it is thought that it cared for its young. At one site, fossils of baby dinos that couldn't yet walk were found. This suggests that, like human babies, they would have needed looking after until they could fend for themselves.

Back legs longer than front legs, so it could stand on two legs, or four

Huge Herds:

Fossils found in Montana, USA, suggest that Maiasauras lived and travelled together in large groups. This would have offered them protection from predatory dinosaurs, such as T-rex, which lived at the same time.

How Many?

Count all the baby Maiasauras on these pages.

There are ☐ babies!

Answers on page 69.

DINOSAUR TERRARIUM

Create a terrarium for your toy dinosaurs.

Ask an adult to help !

YOU WILL NEED

- A deep tray and a shallow dish
- Dinosaur toys
- Leaves, branches and sticks
- Pebbles and stones
- Blue paint and paint brush
- Tin foil
- Water

HOW TO MAKE

1. Collect leaves, branches, sticks, pebbles and stones from a garden or park.

2. Wrap foil around a shallow dish and paint blue (dry).

3. Fill your deep tray with soil and make a hole. Place your painted shallow dish in the hole and fill with water (this is the pond).

4. Add the rocks, leaves and other bits you collected from the garden.

5. Add your toy dinosaurs.

6. If you want, add some speech bubbles to your dinos.

Let's get crafty!

BIG AND SMALL

Just how large were the dinosaurs?

BIG AND SMALL

We know from fossils that some dinosaurs were absolutely enormous, while some were teeny tiny! It's difficult to name the largest and smallest species for certain, as palaeontologists rarely find an entire skeleton.

BIGGEST OF ALL

One of the largest dinosaurs of all time, Argentinosaurus was a colossal creature! It is thought to have reached lengths of up to 35m (114ft).

STEP ON THE SCALES

Plant-eaters were typically MUCH larger than meat-eaters. Giganotosaurus, one of the biggest meat-eaters, weighed around eight tonnes. While that is huge, the biggest plant-eaters could weigh up to 100 tonnes!

Argentinosaurus

TINY DINO

Microraptor is often named as the smallest dinosaur. It was about as large as a chicken, ran around on two legs and hunted smaller animals and insects to eat. In March 2020, an even smaller dino fossil was found trapped in amber. Scientists have named it Oculudentavis khaungraae, which means "unusual eye tooth bird". Maybe Microraptor isn't the smallest after all!

Most Deadly

The deadliest dinosaurs were the most efficient hunters – greater bulk and a stronger bite didn't mean more fighting power. Some of the most dangerous dinosaurs were small dinosaurs, like Velociraptor and Coelophysis.

Velociraptor

BIG FOOT

The largest dino footprints discovered so far are 1.7m (5.5ft) in length, whereas the smallest yet discovered are about 1cm (0.4in) long. Experts don't know if they came from a new species or if they belonged to a baby dino.

ARGENTINOSAURUS

May have been the biggest land animal to ever walk the Earth.

Biggest of All

Argentinosaurus is one of the largest dinosaurs ever discovered. Only a few of its remains have been found, but one of these, a lower leg bone, is more than 1.5m (60in) long. That's absolutely ENORMOUS!

Long neck

DINO FACTS

Name: *Argentinosaurus*

Meaning: *"Argentina lizard"*

Size comparison:

Food: *Plants*

Danger rating: *4/10*

Habitat: *Forests*

How Heavy?

Experts believe that Argentinosaurus could have weighed up to 100 tonnes as a fully grown adult. That's almost as heavy as a blue whale. Its babies are thought to have weighed much less – only 5kg (11lb)!

CRUNCH

Huge body

Large Appetite

This huge dinosaur would have eaten massive amounts of food to fuel its bulky body. It spent its days munching on conifer trees with its thin teeth. Experts estimate that it would have needed to eat an amazing 100,000 calories in a single day. That's almost 40 times as much as an adult human eats in the same amount of time!

Heavy tail

Alpha-Saurus

How many 3, 4 and 5-letter words can you find in

DINOSAUR?

Answers on page 69.

WATCH YOUR STEP!

Whose footprints are these?
Follow the footprints to find the dinosaur that made them.

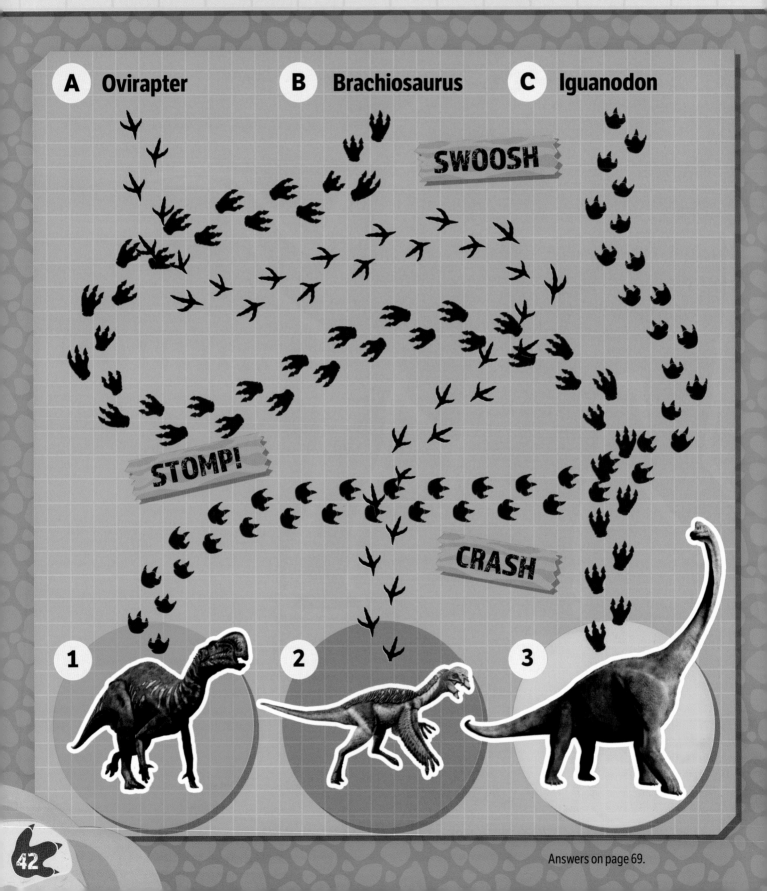

A Ovirapter

B Brachiosaurus

C Iguanodon

SWOOSH

STOMP!

CRASH

1

2

3

Answers on page 69.

Brachiosaurus

Glossary box:
Fossilised footprints are called **ichnites**.

Ask an adult to help !

Footprint Paints

Can you create your own prehistoric footprints? Use your feet as brushes and get stomping!

Lay newspaper on the ground then carefully paint the bottom of your feet using a paintbrush. Step onto plain paper to leave your footprint, then when it is dry, measure it with a ruler. Try using different colours, and don't forget to wash your feet!

Stomp! Stomp! Brachiosaurus had the largest footprint ever recorded, measuring over 1m (3ft)!

Did You Know

To work out which kind of dinosaur a footprint belongs to, scientists consider where it was found and also the kind of rock it formed in. They also look at the size and shape of the markings, as well as how many prints there are.

Iguanodon

43

MICRORAPTOR

This dinosaur was a tiny terror!

Tiny Dino:

Microraptor was one of the tiniest dinosaurs of all – it weighed just one kilogram (2.2 lb), which is about the same as a guinea pig!

DINO FACTS

Name: *Microraptor*

Meaning: *"Tiny plunderer"*

Size comparison:

Food: *Meat*

Danger rating: *5/10*

Habitat: *Woodlands near water*

Sounds Fishy

Fossil remains show that this small dinosaur mostly ate fish, though it would have also eaten small land mammals and birds, too.

Did You Know:

More than 300 Microraptor fossils have been found – that's a lot more than many other kinds of dinosaur!

Feathery Legs:

Fossil remains of Microrapter discovered in China in 2000 showed that it had long feathers on both its arms and legs. It is unlikely that Microraptor could fly very well, yet it may have launched itself into the air and glided for short distances, perhaps between trees.

Get Colouring

Draw more feathers on this Microraptor's head, chest and tail, then colour it in!

FINDING FOSSILS

Experts often go on expeditions to the desert to find fossils.
Can you find all the fossils?

Write how many of each fossil here

Answers on page 69.

How many of each fossil can you find?

47

CARNIVORE vs HERBIVORE

It's all in the diet!

One way to group dinosaurs is to split them up by what, and how, they eat. As you may already know, carnivores eat meat and herbivores eat plants, but how can we tell which dinosaurs ate what millions of year later?

THEIR TEETH

Carnivores are more likely to have zigzag shaped or extremely sharp teeth for cutting through their prey. Herbivores tend to have multiple rows of teeth, some which are round like spoons, perfect for ripping leaves from branches.

SMALL AND FAST

Troodon

THEIR BRAINS

The part of the brain that responds to smell is bigger in carnivores so that they can sniff out their prey.

Diplodocus

Did You Know?

Did you know some dinosaurs have been discovered without teeth? This makes it nearly impossible for palaeontologists to figure out what they ate!

BIG AND SLOW

THEIR STOMACHS

Stones have been found in the stomachs of dinosaurs such as Diplodocus. These stones would have aided the digestion of large amounts of vegetation.

THEIR EYES

Carnivorous dinos had bigger eyes that faced slightly forward. This would have aided them in hunting.

THEIR POO

Some fossils of poo can be used to determine the dinosaur's last meal. For example, small bones were found in a Tyrannosarus rex's droppings — ew!

49

STEGOSAURUS

This dino was a self-defence superstar.

Tiny brain

Two rows of bony plates

Pretty Plates

Stegosaurus is one of the best-known dinosaurs of all time. It is easily recognised by the rows of large bony plates that ran down its back. These plates were quite thin, so it is unlikely they were used in self-defence.

Tail Spikes

If it came under attack, Stegosaurus used the sharp spikes at the end of its tail to bash away predators, such as Allosaurus. Allosaurus fossils have been found with large holes thought to be made by a Stegosaurus spike. **Ouch!**

Spiky tail

Did You Know:

Stegosaurus had a tiny brain despite its large size. It wasn't the most intelligent of the dinosaurs!

CHOMP!

Plants for Dinner

This dino had a beak, which it used to eat ferns and other low-lying plants such as moss. **Chomp chomp!**

DINO FACTS

Name: *Stegosaurus*

Meaning: *"Roof lizard"*

Size comparison:

Food: *Plants*

Danger rating: *5/10*

Habitat: *Floodplains and grasslands*

Spot the Stegosaurus

Which of these dinos is a Stegosaurus?

Answers on page 69.

DINO WORD SEARCH

Can you find all the dinosaur words hidden in the grid?

T	R	O	T	P	A	R	D	D	F
C	S	R	E	P	T	I	L	E	O
N	W	C	B	N	N	Y	R	W	S
I	A	U	I	O	A	E	O	B	S
T	L	E	S	S	N	C	U	Q	I
X	C	A	A	Z	S	E	Z	V	L
E	U	C	I	S	S	A	R	U	J
R	T	E	E	T	H	F	I	H	T
T	B	J	C	G	M	P	Y	R	F
J	U	B	D	X	R	F	T	H	T

- BONE
- CLAWS
- DINOSAUR
- EXTINCT
- FOSSIL
- JURASSIC
- RAPTOR
- REPTILE
- TEETH
- TRIASSIC

Answers on page 69.

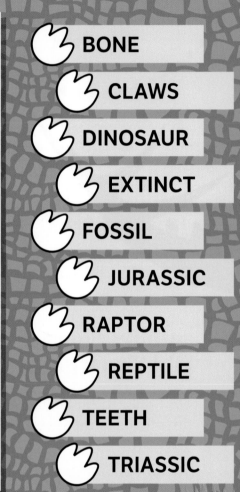

Colour in a dinosaur footprint each time you find the word!

52

JOIN THE DOTS!

Complete the dot-to-dots to finish the pictures of these deadly dinos, then colour them in! Can you name each dinosaur?

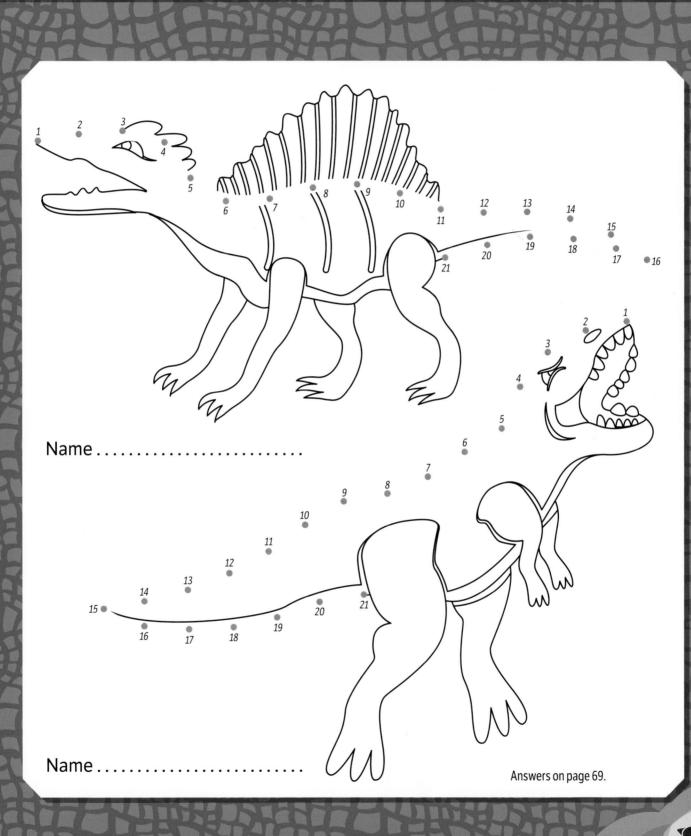

Name . . . .

Name . . . .

Answers on page 69.

53

DEINONYCHUS

This dino used its deadly claws to strike prey.

DINO FACTS

Name: *Deinonychus*

Meaning: *"Terrible claw"*

Size comparison:

Food: *Meat*

Danger rating: *9/10*

Habitat: *Swampy or tropical forests*

Did You Know:

Deinonychus was a sharp-clawed, meat-eating dino that grew to around 3.4m (11ft) in length. It was a distant relative of the famous hunter, Velociraptor.

Pack Hunter

Deinonychus may have hunted in packs, attacking dinosaurs as large as the plant-eating Tenontosaurus. Fossils of both dinos have been found together.

Clever Creature

It had a large brain compared to its body size, suggesting it was an intelligent dinosaur.

SNARL

Blade-like teeth

Terrible Claw

This lightly built predator wounded its prey using a large claw on either foot. Its jaw strength was quite poor, which probably means it relied solely on its talons for hunting.

Most likely had feathers

Sharp claws

It's All in the Name!

Hint: What body part gave Deinonychus its name?

TERIBERL CWAL

Answers on page 69.

CAMOUFLAGED CARNIVORES

Can you spot all the meat-eating dinosaurs in this prehistoric scene?
How many of each carnivorous dinosaur can you find?

Hint: Check behind the leaves!

Write how many of each carnivore here

Answers on page 69.

FEATHERS AND SCALES

How do we know what dinos looked like?

DINO SKIN

For many years, it was thought that all dinosaurs had scaly skin, like a reptile, yet evidence shows that many dinosaurs had feathers.

IN THE FAMILY

Even though it sounds far-fetched, experts now agree that birds developed from the theropod dinosaur family, which included T-rex!

FLIGHTLESS:
Even though some dinosaurs had feathers, they probably couldn't fly like a modern-day bird. Their body structure couldn't support flight. They may have used the feathers to keep warm or to impress potential mates instead!

WHICH IS CORRECT?
This artist has drawn T-rex with feathers, while another artist has shown it with scales.

Which one do you think is correct?

Answers on page 69.

ARCHAEOPTERYX

The link between dinosaurs and birds.

DINO FACTS

Name: *Archaeopteryx*

Meaning: *"Ancient wing"*

Size comparison:

Food: *Meat*

Danger rating: *6/10*

Habitat: *Swampy or tropical forests*

SCREECH!

Still a Dino

Just like modern-day birds, Archaeopteryx had a light skeleton, yet it still had many dinosaur features – such as sharp teeth, a bony tail and claws on its wings.

Short Flights

It is unlikely that Archaeopteryx could fly very well – but it may have been able to travel short distances in bursts, a bit like a pheasant!

First Bird

Archaeopteryx was the first bird-like dino to be discovered. Its fossil remains were found in Germany in the mid-1800s. They clearly showed that this raven-sized creature had feathers.

Glossary box:
The first airborne dinos were called **avalians**.

Bony jaw

Deadly claws

Feathers on legs and wings

LET'S COUNT!

Each dinosaur represents a number.
Can you solve the puzzles?

= 1   = 2   = 3   = 4

A   + = ?

B   + = ?

C   + = ?

D   + = ?

Answers on page 69.

62

ALL IN A MUDDLE!

These dinosaurs are jumbled up!
How many of each dinosaur can you count?

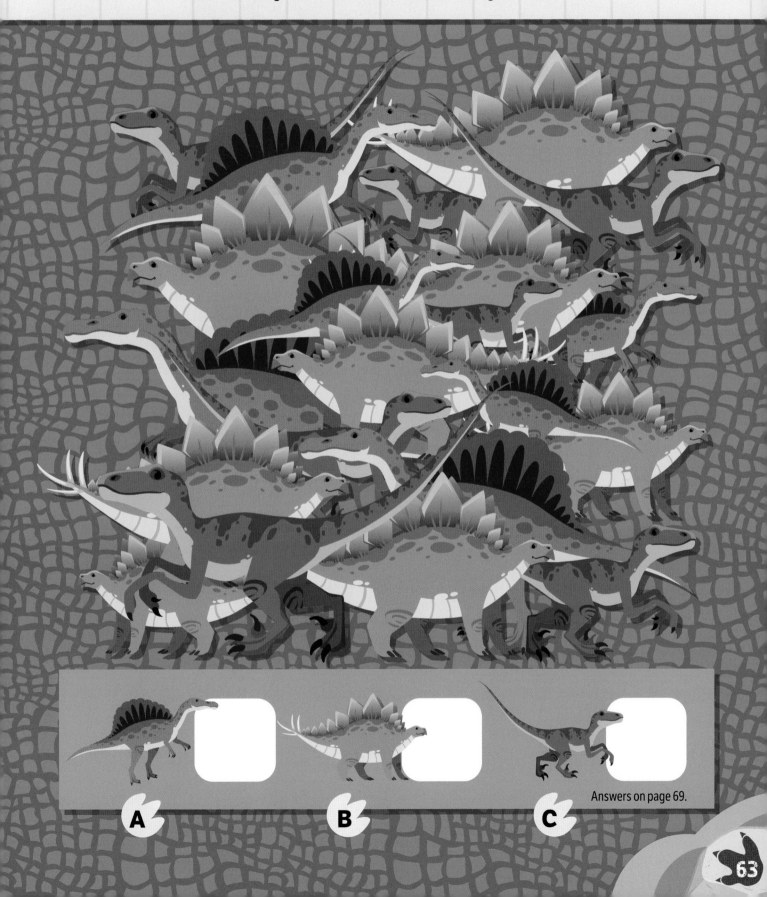

A

B

C

Answers on page 69.

ANKYLOSAURUS

This dino is known for its awesome armour.

DINO FACTS

Name: *Ankylosaurus*

Meaning: *"Stiff lizard"*

Size comparison:

Food: *Plants*

Danger rating: *6/10*

Habitat: *Floodplains*

Did You Know

Many plant-eating dinosaurs had front legs that were shorter than its back legs. This helped them get close to the leaves and plants on the ground.

Chomp!

Ankylosaurus ate low-lying plants using its narrow beak, swallowing leaves without chewing them properly. The leaves were then broken down in its digestive system.

Bulky body

RUMBLE

Fused Together

The top of this heavily armoured dinosaur was covered in thick plates and rows of spikes to protect it from predators. Parts of its skeleton, including its skull, were fused together – giving it its name.

Colour in the Dinosaur

We don't know exactly what colours the dinosaurs were. What do you think it looked like?

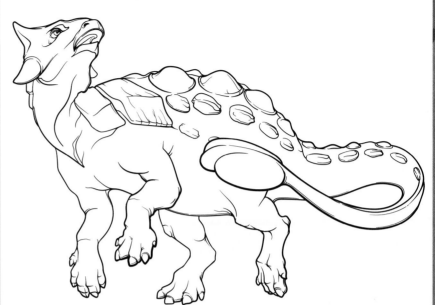

Armoured plates

Club on end of tail

Rows of spikes

BANG

Club Tail

If an Ankylosaurus came under attack, it would use its large club tail to knock predators away.

65

WHO AM I ?

Read the clues and study the dinosaurs.
Can you work out who they are?

1 I was a tyrant lizard

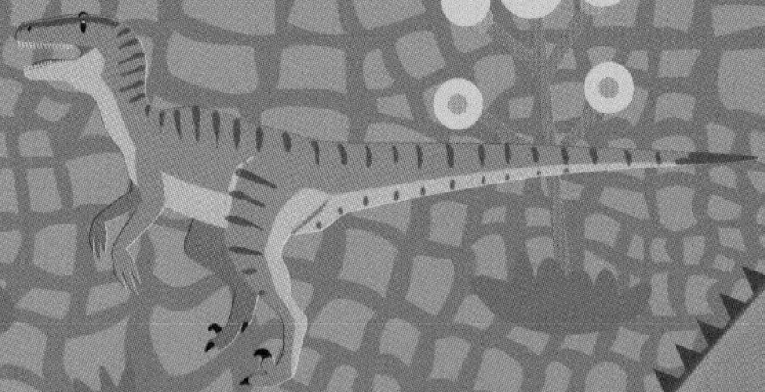

2 I could run very fast

3 I was over 26m long

4 I was a self-defense superstar

5 I was unlike any other dinosaur

6 My bony plates were fused together

Answers on page 69.

QUIZ TIME!

True or False?

1. Triceratops had two horns on its face.

2. T-rex's diet was made up of plants, such as ferns.

3. Diplodocus was one of the first dinosaurs to have feathers.

4. The name Velociraptor means "quick plunderer".

5. The word dinosaur means "lovely lizard".

Test your memory!

1. What is the name of the smallest dinosaur?

2. What is a fossilised footprint called?

3. Which dinosaur's name means "tyrant lizard"?

4. At the end of which time period did the dinosaurs become extinct?

5. How fast do scientists believe Velociraptor could run?

ANSWERS

p.11 Dino Close-Ups
Picture **2** is from an Iguanodon

p.12–13 Spot the Difference!

p.15 True or False? - False – Diplodocus ate plants

p.19 Guess the Name! - D. Scientists named it
Vectaerovenator inopinatus, which means "air-filled
hunter from the Isle of Wight" (where it was found)

p.21 Track the Trail - Trail C.

p.26-27 Prehistoric Puzzlers
1. A Thesaurus! **2.** A terror-dactyl!
3. On his tricera-bottom! **4.** You are a sight for saur-eyes!
5. Banter-saurus! **6.** A nervous Rex

p.31 All Mixed Up - Piece C.

p.32 A-Maze-ing Discovery!

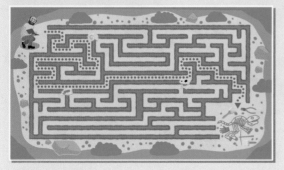

p.35 How Many?
There are 7 babies

p.41 Alpha-Saurus
Here are some words you may have found: and, air, drain,
nod, our, radio, ran, road, round, son, sound, sour, sun

p.42 Watch Your Step!
A. Ovirapter - **2.** B. Brachiosaurus - **3.** C. Iguanodon - **1.**

p.46 Finding Fossils

p.51 Spot the Stegosaurus   **p.52 Dino Word Search**

p.53 Join the Dots!
Spinosaurus and T-Rex

p.55 It's all in the name! - TERRIBLE CLAW

p.56 Camouflaged Carnivores

p.62 Let's Count! - **a** = 3, **b** = 7, **c** = 5, **d** = 5

p.63 All in a Muddle! - **a** = 6, **b** = 8, **c** = 7

p.66-67 Who Am I ?
1. T-Rex **2.** Velociraptor **3.** Diplodocus
4. Stegosaurus **5.** Allosaurus **6.** Ankylosaurus

p.68 Quiz Time!

True or False?
1. False – it had three horns
2. False – T-Rex was a meat-eater
3. False – Diplodocus didn't have any feathers
4. True – Velocirator does mean "quick plunderer"
5. False – dinosaur means terrible lizard

Test your memory!
1. Microraptor
2. Ichnites
3. T-rex
4. The Cretaceous Period
5. 40 mph (60 km/h)